Jan was washing her hair and had managed to get shampoo in her eyes. "Ouch, that stings!" she yelped. She jumped out of the shower area and started feeling around blindly on the bench where she had left her towel. "Hey, guys, come on," she pleaded. "Where'd you put my stuff?"

"We didn't do anything—" Sara began.

"Yikes!" Amy interrupted her. She had stepped out of the shower and was surveying the row of dressing stalls. "Everything's gone! Someone stole our things! What are we going to do?"

Other books about the Fifth Grade Stars:

Fifth Grade S·T·A·R·S

CRAZY CAMPOUT

By Lisa Norby

Bullseye Books · Alfred A. Knopf
New York

For Kirsten

DR. M. JERRY WEISS, Distinguished Service Professor of Communications at Jersey City State College, is the educational consultant for Bullseye Books. Currently chair of the International Reading Association President's Advisory Committee on Intellectual Freedom, he travels frequently to give workshops on the use of trade books in schools.

Library of Congress Cataloging-in-Publication Data
Norby, Lisa. Crazy campout / by Lisa Norby.   p.   cm.—
(Bullseye books) (Fifth Grade Stars ; #3) Summary:
The Fifth Grade Stars are excited about a weekend
campout, until they discover a rival clique at the next
campsite.   ISBN 0-394-89607-6 (pbk.)   [1. Camping—
Fiction.   2. Clubs—Fiction.]   I. Title.
II. Series.   PZ7.N7752Cr   1989   [Fic]—dc19
88-14695

RL: 5.8

Manufactured in the United States of America
1 2 3 4 5 6 7 8 9 0

◄ 1 ►
One Weird Weekend

"This is going to be like one of those good news–bad news jokes," Beth Greenfield predicted. "The good news is that this is the warmest October weather on record and we have Monday off for Columbus Day."

"Right," agreed her identical twin, Sara. "And the bad news is that we aren't going anywhere."

It was Thursday afternoon, and the Stars were sitting around in their snug stone clubhouse in the woods, talking about their plans for the coming weekend. Except for Beth and Sara, the girls hadn't known each other long. At the end of the summer, their families had moved into Sugar Tree Acres, the new housing development on the outskirts of River Grove, and the five girls rode the same school bus—the one that had the big sign S.T.A.R. in the front window, for Sugar Tree Acres Road.

By chance, the Stars had all ended up in the same class with Holly Hudnut, the self-appointed princess of their class at River Grove Elementary and the president of the Clovers, the rich girls' club. "If you're in, you're in Clover," the saying went. "And if you're out, forget it."

For some reason, Holly had made up her mind right away that all the kids who rode the S.T.A.R. bus were nerds. That was when Amy Danner had suggested that they fight back by starting a club of their own. And since they all rode the S.T.A.R. route bus, they called themselves the Stars.

Everything had been going great for the club for a few weeks, but now, with the long weekend coming up, the girls were starting to feel sorry for themselves.

"You can bet the Clovers aren't going to be hanging around River Grove this weekend," Amy pointed out. "They have some big plan. They've been whispering and passing notes to each other about it all week long."

"Isn't it awful how everything the Clovers do has to be such a big secret," sighed brown-haired, athletic-looking Jan Bateman. "The worst of it is, they probably *are* going someplace nice. Holly's parents are always organizing trips and stuff. Last summer, Holly got to invite all her friends to her family's beach house for two whole weeks. I heard them talking about it."

"It's not fair," Beth groused. "Sara and I didn't get to go away all summer long. And now the family can't go anywhere because Mom is expecting the baby in a couple of weeks."

Shy, serious Karen Fisher played with a few strands of her blond hair. "Aren't you happy that your mother is having a baby?" she said wistfully. "I think it would be exciting to have a little brother or sister. It gets boring at my house with just me and my parents around."

"Oh, our house is exciting, all right." Beth laughed. "Just last week, Jeffrey and Amanda got into an argument over whether they were going to watch *Laffbusters* or *Sesame Street,* and Jeffrey ended up spilling grape juice in the TV and it made this crackling sound and gave off a puff of smoke. Then later that same day our cat got out onto the roof and got stuck in the rain gutter. The firemen said it was the first time they ever got called to the same house twice in one day."

"Jeffrey called them about the TV," Sara explained to the others. "And poor Clementine did need help. Sometimes she forgets what an old cat she is and gets into situations she can't get out of."

Sara realized that neither of them had answered Karen's question, so she added, "Of course we're happy about the new baby. It's just that our family used to have a lot of fun going on trips together. But we already had a carful with four kids. With five, I don't know how we'll ever go anywhere."

"Your folks aren't the only ones who never go away," Jan said. "My dad has to coach the football team every day after school. And he works every weekend besides. Then when football season is over, he helps out with the track team. My mom says she goes to the games because otherwise she'd forget what he looks like."

"When I grow up, I'm going to marry

someone who has the kind of job where both of us can go a lot of places together. Someone like Sean!" Sara got a dreamy expression on her face.

The other girls looked at her and shook their heads. While the rest of them had been working at cleaning up the clubhouse, Sara had been making notes for the romance novel she was always talking about writing. The main characters were beautiful, sophisticated Tiffany Vandermere—a redhead, like Sara—and her dashing lover, Sean, a former pirate who was trying to go straight. Sometimes Sara got so wrapped up in her stories that she almost forgot Sean and Tiffany weren't real.

"You can all complain, but at least all your dads live at home," Amy said. She'd tried to sound casual, but her voice had a bitter edge to it.

For a moment no one said anything. Amy's parents were divorced, and her dad lived in another state. She hardly ever mentioned him, and this was the first time they had ever had a hint that she was upset about his not being around. But then, Amy wasn't one to show her inner feelings.

In fact, sometimes you even forgot to

wonder about the inner Amy, because the outer Amy was such a character. She loved colorful clothes and offbeat jewelry. At the moment, she happened to be dressed— tamely by her standards—in a Mickey Mouse T-shirt and white painter's pants with pockets all the way down the legs. Her high-top sneakers were decorated with embroidered patches she had sewn on, and dozens of tiny braids stuck out all around her head like a porcupine's quills. Amy was convinced that if she wore the braids long enough, her hair would eventually become permanently curly, though why she wanted frizzy hair in the first place was a mystery to Beth and Sara. They would have given anything to exchange their wiry red mops for Amy's nice, straight brown hair.

Amy had been lying on some cushions on the floor, with her feet propped up on the arms of the old easy chair where Jan was sitting. Suddenly she stood up and began pacing around the tiny clubhouse. Her face was a funny, tomatoey shade.

At first, the other girls assumed that Amy's red face was caused by her lying with her feet in the air. But Jan saw that Amy was upset. Of course, they'd all been pretty tactless to sit around complaining about their families in front of her. At least they all had both parents at home, which made them luckier than a lot of the kids in their class.

"I'm sorry," Jan apologized. "I guess I forgot that you never get to see your dad at all. That must be tough."

"Oh, I'm going to see him, all right," Amy said angrily. "He's coming tomorrow to pick me up. We're going camping for the whole weekend at Lake Laverne."

The other girls exchanged looks of confusion.

"I don't get it," said Karen. "Why does it make you mad that your dad is going to take you camping? Is he really so awful that you don't want to see him?"

"Nah, I guess not." Amy picked at a loose piece of the latex Mickey Mouse design on her shirt. "He's a regular dad. You know. It's just that he makes me uncomfortable. I don't know what we'll say to each other all weekend."

Amy looked as if she hoped they'd change the subject, so Karen did. "I wish I knew where the Clovers are going," she said.

"Don't worry," said Jan. "Wherever they

go, you can bet we'll hear all about it later. You know how Holly loves to brag."

Holly's parents had loads of money, and her mom was a big wheel in town because she was president of the River Grove Preservation Society. Holly herself was pretty in a blond, blue-eyed, doll-like sort of way, but she was a creep. She loved to boss the other Clovers around. If she wore preppy clothes to school, you could be sure all the Clovers would immediately stock up on alligator shirts and Top-Siders. And ever since Holly started wearing her hair pulled into a side ponytail, all the others did too, no matter how dumb it looked.

"Oh, well," sighed Karen. "So who cares about the stupid Clovers. At least we're getting a long weekend. And the original version of *Invasion of the Body Snatchers* is going to be on TV on Saturday afternoon. I've seen it four times, but I can always go for number five."

"Right," agreed Jan. "And I can always try out some new recipes. I think my mom is just about ready to give in and let me make this okra soup that Chef Hubert demonstrated on his TV show last week."

"Yuck!" Amy made a face. "I think cooking is kind of a strange hobby anyway, but at least you could make good stuff. Like a chocolate cake or something. Why okra?"

"I don't know." Jan shrugged. She hadn't really thought about it before, but maybe cooking exotic foods was something she did when she got tired of being nice, normal Jan Bateman. Everything else about her was so . . . well, average. Average height. Average looks. Average brown hair. Average grades. "I guess I just like being different," she said aloud. "Anyway, it's fun to see my folks' reactions. A lot of times they like what I make, but they never think they will ahead of time."

"Well, I still wish we could go away," Beth said. "It would be a lot more fun to go camping with Amy's dad."

"Somehow I think he'd notice the switch if you showed up instead of me," Amy said. "Although it's been so long since I've seen him that maybe he wouldn't even catch on."

"No, wait. I'm serious," Beth insisted. "Why don't you ask your dad if we can all come along? We could bring our own sleeping bags. We'd have a lot of fun. And it would save you from having to find stuff to talk to your dad about for a whole weekend. I mean, he'll probably say no. But it couldn't hurt to ask."

Amy was caught by surprise. None of the girls had met her dad, and none of them knew how tough things had been for her last year when her parents split up. Amy wasn't sure she was ready to let her friends learn about that part of her life. On the other hand, a group trip might be more fun. Beth's idea was sounding better and better. It was true: having company around should make getting along with her dad easier.

"Why not?" she said aloud. "My dad has a van. So there'd be plenty of room for all of us. But are you all sure you want to spend a long weekend with him? He can be a little weird sometimes."

"I'd put up with Godzilla for a chance to go away this weekend," Beth said. "Besides, how could anyone *not* have a good time on a camping trip?"

Karen Fisher thought she knew.

When Karen and her parents went on vacation, they stayed in luxury hotels, complete with heated pools, health spas, and room service breakfasts. "Does this mean we'd have to sleep outside on the bare ground? And go all weekend without a bathroom?" she asked warily.

"Of course not," Amy said. For the brain of the group, Karen sometimes didn't know the most obvious things. "The campground has bathrooms and showers. They're kind of primitive. But they're there."

"Oh, right," said Karen. She wasn't sure exactly how "primitive" Amy meant, but she decided she'd just as soon not know the details.

"And we'd sleep in tents," Jan put in. "My brother has a big tent that's almost brand-new. He'd probably let me borrow it. Especially if it meant getting out of having okra soup for dinner on Saturday."

"Okay," said Amy uncertainly. "I'll call my dad tonight and ask him. Why not?"

By the time Amy phoned her father that evening, she had convinced herself that he would say no. But to her surprise, he thought inviting the Stars along on the trip was a great idea. "I've never met any of your friends in River Grove," he said. "In fact, I'm flattered that you want them to meet me."

"I wouldn't go that far," said Amy.

Her dad laughed. "That's my girl. Always a kidder."

Why is it that when you tell the truth, that's exactly when adults think you're kidding? Amy wondered. But before she could say anything more, her father asked to talk to her mom, so he could get the phone numbers of the other girls' parents.

For the rest of the evening, the phone lines connecting the Stars' houses buzzed with activity. It seemed to take about a million calls to get everything organized, but by bedtime the trip was all arranged.

At the Greenfield house, Sara was already beginning to have second thoughts. "Next time, consult me before you come out with one of your brilliant plans," she told Beth as she pushed their Labrador retriever off her bed so that she could crawl into it. "What if Amy's dad turns out to be really mean? We'll be stuck with him for a whole weekend."

And at the Bateman house, Jan was feeling a little nervous too. She picked up the phone and dialed Karen Fisher. "Amy seemed upset when she talked about her dad," Jan reminded Karen. "What if he and Amy fight all the time? This could be one weird weekend."

"You said it," Karen agreed. "But it's not Amy's dad I'm worried about. It's snakes and spiders and stuff like that."

Jan was surprised. Karen was the smartest of all the Stars. Surely she couldn't be afraid of something as silly as a spider.

"You aren't really scared of animals, are you?" Jan asked.

"Of course not. I love animals. It's just that I'm not sure how I feel about sleeping out there in the woods with them. It would be awfully creepy to wake up and see some big rattlesnake staring you right in the eyes."

Jan laughed. "Rattlesnakes at Lake Laverne—that's a good one! For a minute there, I thought you were serious. You sounded just like some little kid who's never been to camp before."

Karen was glad that Jan couldn't see the nervous expression on her face. Just because she was tall and got good grades in school, people always expected her to act older than her age. That had its advantages, of course. Her parents treated her almost as if she were a grownup, and they got along just fine.

In school, though, she sometimes wished she were small and cute-looking, like the Greenfield twins. No one seemed surprised when Beth and Sara needed help. But every time Karen Fisher admitted she was upset or uncertain, or just scared of something, someone would accuse her of "acting like a little kid."

No one ever seems to notice that I *am* still a kid, Karen thought a bit resentfully. Just because I'm not so little, that doesn't mean that I don't have problems too.

But even now, talking to Jan, Karen felt a little bit silly asking for advice. "I never *have* been to camp," she admitted with an embarrassed giggle. "But so what? What could there be to know?"

"That's right," Jan added confidently. "I'm sure we'll all have a great time. After all, it's just a three-day trip. What could go wrong?"

◀ 2 ▶
Lake Laverne, Here We Come!

"Lake Laverne, here we come!" exclaimed Amy's dad as he started up the van and headed down Janice Drive.

He had popped a cassette of old Beatles songs into the dashboard tape player, and soon he was singing along happily. "We all live in a yellow submarine, yellow submarine, yellow submarine . . ."

In the middle seat of the van, Beth poked Sara in the ribs and rolled her eyes toward the ceiling. Sara stifled a giggle.

"When Amy said her father was a little weird, she wasn't kidding," Jan whispered to Karen, who was sitting next to her in the rear seat.

"And I thought she said that she and her dad had nothing in common," Karen whispered back. "If you ask me, they're alike. Sort of."

Mr. Danner had a reddish beard and a big stomach, and he looked like a cross between a teddy bear and one of the hippies that Jan had seen on TV in a show about what things were like back in the sixties. His hair was shiny and clean, but he wore it so long that he had pulled it back with a rubber band into a little ponytail.

When he stopped off to pick up each of the girls and meet their parents, Mr. Danner had been wearing a sports coat and tie, the kind of clothes he wore to his job as a computer programmer. Before they left, though, he had changed into his camping clothes—a bizarre combination that included painter's pants covered from mid-thigh to waist with a dozen or more baggy pockets, like Amy's, and a red-and-black football shirt under a clashing yellow-and-green-plaid shirt.

Karen was right, Jan thought. It was no

wonder Amy thought Day-Glo orange and pink was a quiet color combination. Compared to her dad's, Amy's taste in clothes was almost conservative.

Jan tried to decide how old Mr. Danner was, but it was awfully hard to tell. His beard made him look like an old man at first glance. And probably he was quite a bit older than her dad. But he acted young. He seemed excited about the camping trip, almost more excited than the girls were.

During the whole ride, he kept feeding tapes into the player and singing along to the music. At first, everyone was too embarrassed to join in. Then Beth and Jan started to sing along too, and soon they were all singing, with Karen and Sara picking out the alto harmonies and Mr. Danner adding the booming bass notes.

Amy was the only one not singing. As soon as her father started playing tapes, she had decided that the trip was a big mistake. When she was little, she had always enjoyed singing along with her dad. But now she was embarrassed. She was sure the others thought he was being silly, even though they acted as if they were having a good time. Her friends were probably just pretending, to be polite, Amy figured.

Her dad's clothes were embarrassing too. It's one thing for me to dress creatively, Amy told herself. But her father was a grownup. Her dad had been a musician, and he had a lot of friends who dressed in ways that were sort of, well, out of the ordinary. That hadn't bothered her when they lived in New York. But in Sugar Tree Acres, none of the fathers looked like that. None of them had beards, or long hair. Why couldn't he be more like the other fathers? Amy slunk down in her seat and stared out the windshield, frowning.

An hour and a half later, they arrived at the campground. A big sign over the entrance announced: KEMPER'S KAMPGROUND, LAKESIDE SITES ON LAKE LAVERNE.

"There's a tongue twister for you," said Mr. Danner. "Try to say that five times fast." And since they were all feeling slightly silly by then, they all did try. All except Amy.

When they got inside the log cabin office, the woman at the registration desk took out a map of the grounds and drew an "X" over site number 29, the one that was reserved for them. "We're not too crowded at this time of year, so you have one of our loveliest sites," she told them.

They drove around the long, looping road that circled the grounds, until finally Amy spotted their number. The site was surrounded on three sides by pine trees and tall boulders. On the fourth side, just beyond another empty campsite, lay Lake Laverne, its waters shimmering in the early evening light.

"It *is* beautiful!" Sara said, in awe at the sight.

A chipmunk sitting on the picnic table chattered a loud welcome.

"Hey, Karen, watch out!" teased Jan. "It's a wild animal! Jump in the car and roll up the windows."

"Be serious," Karen said, mildly embarrassed. "I'm not scared of chipmunks."

Now that they were out of the van and there was work to do, Amy's spirits rose. "Come on, guys," she said. "We still have an hour or so before it gets dark. Let's use the time to get our tent set up and dinner started."

Beth helped Jan unload the big box that was marked "5-Person Geodesic Tent." Inside it they found yards and yards of silver and purple nylon and more than a dozen pieces of aluminum tubing.

"Now what?" asked Beth, staring helplessly at the sea of nylon.

Amy's dad looked over the jumble and scratched his head. "Beats me," he said. "But I bet by the time I get the van unloaded and my own tent set up, you girls will have figured it all out."

Sara had found the instructions and was reading them out loud: " 'Thread the ferrule of tent pole 1-A through the corresponding sleeve.' " She looked around. "Does anybody know what a ferrule is?"

"Here, let me try." Karen started studying the instructions. Maybe she didn't know anything about camping, but she was usually pretty good at figuring out how to assemble things. Before long, she and the twins had the parts of the tent all laid out on the ground in the right order and were systematically fitting them together.

Meanwhile, Jan was rummaging through all the gear that had been on the roof rack, looking for food. "I volunteer to make dinner," she yelled to the others. "But where's the box of groceries? I thought you said you were bringing stuff, but I don't see anything here."

Amy came over to the van. "Here it is," she told Jan. "You're looking right at it."

Jan started looking through the box Amy was pointing at. " 'Freeze-dried macaroni and cheese.' 'Freeze-dried beef stew.' 'Freeze-dried eggs.' . . . What *is* this stuff?"

"This is what we ate at the wilderness survival camp I went to last summer," Amy explained. "It's not bad when you get used to it."

"But you were backpacking then, right? I mean, we have the van now. We don't need stuff like this."

Amy shrugged. "I know. But I thought it would be fun."

Jan was horrified. Ever since she'd known the trip was on for sure, she'd been thinking about the great outdoor meals she could whip up at the campsite. Fortunately, she'd brought her own emergency supply of cooking aids—spices, Parmesan cheese, even some fresh tomatoes.

Looking through the rest of the gear, she discovered that Amy's dad had brought a stash of food too. His shopping bags contained jumbo-size jars of peanut butter and grape jelly, Sugar Snax cereal, several kinds of cookies, a box of double-chocolate brownies, marshmallows for toasting over the fire, and two giant bags of potato chips.

Jan let out a low whistle. "I thought your mom was opposed to sugar!"

"She is," Amy said. "But my dad is the junk-food king."

Mr. Danner overheard. "I remember how you always loved chocolate. Anyway, you're on vacation. It won't hurt you to have sweets for a couple of days."

"Mom won't like it," Amy said automatically.

"Well, your mother isn't here. And what she doesn't know won't hurt her."

Amy knew she'd said something wrong, and she wasn't even sure why she'd said it. The fact was, she did love chocolate. In the old days, before her parents got divorced, her dad used to take her side and talk Mom into letting her have a chocolate sundae every once in a while. Then, suddenly, he wasn't around to do that, and Amy was stuck with her mother's super-strict food rules.

Now she was here with her dad, and the rules were off again, but instead of being happy, she had started defending her mom. Amy didn't know if she was angry or just confused. She shrugged her shoulders and went back to helping unpack the van.

Jan, meanwhile, dug deeper into the shopping bags and managed to find a couple of cans of tuna buried under the snack food. She started figuring out how she was going to combine them with some of her spices to make a macaroni casserole. Amy's dad started the stove, put water on to boil, and laid a campfire. Then he helped Karen and the twins finish setting up the tent.

Jan's hero Chef Hubert might not have thought much of the dinner, but by the time it was ready, everyone was so hungry that it tasted delicious.

"Amy's mom and I grew up in this area," Mr. Danner told the girls as they dug into their second helpings. "And I used to come up here to the lake with my brothers on fishing trips. There's nothing better than fishing all day and then eating your own catch for dinner, cooked over an open fire. We used to stay up here a whole week, with just our sleeping bags and some canned food. No watches. No radios. No contact with the outside world.

"Of course," he added, "the part I liked best was hiking up Mount Jasper. There's an old swinging bridge across the stream up there, built by one of the first settlers on this lake. And an Indian cave too. My brothers and I used to call that our secret place."

"Really!" Sara was impressed. She was always thinking up new episodes for her novel. "It would be really neat if Tiffany and Sean got marooned here for a year and had to survive on wild plants and berries and stuff," she said dreamily.

Beth made a face. "How could you get marooned on the shore of a lake? You need an island to get marooned."

Mr. Danner looked confused. "Who're Tiffany and Sean?"

Everyone laughed, but when Sara explained that they were characters in the novel she was trying to write, Amy's father nodded his head. "Sounds interesting. When you're a famous author, can I have your autograph?"

"Sure." Sara glowed. Amy's dad might be a little strange, but she liked him. Most adults thought her novel was a big joke.

Everyone agreed that Jan's casserole was good, even if it was a little on the spicy side. "Boy, I wish we had some bug juice," said Beth. "I bet I could drink about a gallon of it right now."

"Bug juice!" Karen made a face. "What's that?"

"I thought everyone in the world knew what bug juice is," Beth said. She grinned mischievously. "It's made of all sorts of ground-up beetles and stuff. They give it to you at camp because it's supposed to make you fall asleep fast at night so you don't bother the counselors."

Karen knew she was being teased. "Oh, right," she said. She still wondered what bug juice was, but she didn't dare ask again. Karen wished that she'd never admitted to not knowing anything about camping.

When the last bite of the casserole was finished, they tore into the brownies, then found some sticks and started toasting marshmallows over the campfire.

They were just biting into the first gooey mouthfuls when they heard an eerie cackling from across the lake.

A-whoop—oo-oo-oo!

"What was *that?*" Karen asked.

"A great horned owl, I think," said Mr. Danner.

Karen shivered. "I thought owls were supposed to be wise and friendly. That was spooky. It sounded like a ghost."

"That was nothing." Amy laughed. "Where I went to camp in Canada, they had loons. The first night I was there, the other kids convinced me that the sound they made was a pack of wolves howling. I was really scared."

Amy's dad explained that a loon was a bird that lived by diving for fish. "Sometimes their call does sound almost like a wolf. You weren't the first one to fall for that joke."

"That reminds me," said Jan, "of this story we used to tell at the camp I went to. This guy is camping out by the shore of a lake, sort of like this one, and he hears this horrible screaming that keeps him awake all night long. So the next day, when he goes into town for supplies, he asks what it was, and the storekeeper says, 'Oh, that was the loon.'

"So the guy doesn't worry anymore until

the next night, when he hears the screaming again, worse than before.

"The next day, he goes back to town and
he asks about the noise again. 'I told
you, that's the loon,' says the storekeeper.

"On the third night, the guy hears the
screaming, and it's louder than ever. He sits
up and reaches for his flashlight and turns
it on. And there, standing right over him,
is this horrible *thing*—a creature with
bloodshot eyes, drooling lips, and matted
hair. And in his right hand he's holding a
knife as big as a machete. . . ."

Sara sucked in her breath sharply.
Everyone else was staring at Jan, open-
mouthed. "So what happened?" demanded
Karen.

"Well," Jan continued, "the guy panics.
He jumps out of his sleeping bag and runs
as fast as he can, until he comes to the
general store. Then he pounds on the door
until the owner wakes up and lets him in.
'I thought you said that noise was made by
a loon,' he says to the storekeeper.

"And the storekeeper just stares at him.
'Of course I did. You wouldn't call a person

who goes around murdering campers normal!' "

"Arrrgh!" Beth clutched her throat and lobbed a pillow at Jan.

"That's not fair," Sara protested. "I was in the mood for a scary story, and that turned out to be a joke. And a pretty dumb one, too."

"If it's a scary story you want," Jan said, "I know plenty of those." She leaned forward so that the firelight cast eerie shadows across her face. "Did you ever hear the one about the monkey's paw? . . ."

◀ 3 ▶
The Humongous Blue Camper

Later that night, Karen awoke from a sound sleep.

At least she thought she was awake. It was so dark inside the tent that she could hardly tell whether her eyes were open or not.

She could hear a muffled roar, and a crunching noise made by something heavy moving over the gravel road that ran next to their campsite. Whatever it was, it was no owl. Not unless owls were a lot bigger than she thought!

Tentatively, she lifted a corner of the flap that covered one of the tent's nylon screen windows. Outside was a monster, all right, but not one of the animal variety. A humongous blue camper was inching its way down the narrow, tree-lined road.

As the camper came closer, its headlights raked over the Stars' tent. The light was so bright that Karen could have counted Sara and Beth's freckles. Somehow, the other girls didn't wake up.

Karen looked at her watch. It was only ten thirty. After cleaning up from dinner and trading ghost stories around the fire, everyone had been so sleepy that they had gone to bed early. Now that she was awake, though, Karen knew it wouldn't be easy for her to get back to sleep. Not until the noise stopped. Impatiently, she propped herself up on one elbow and stared through the tent flap at the noisy camper, belching smelly exhaust fumes.

The driver was trying to back into the campsite that lay directly between the Stars' tent and the shore of the lake. He was having a terrible time, because the camper was so wide.

Gross! Karen thought. Now that ugly thing is going to block our view of the lake for the rest of the weekend.

She noticed that a light had come on in the rear of the camper. Out of curiosity, she raised the tent flap a little higher and peered out, trying to get a look at their new neighbors.

At first, all she saw was the back view of a woman wearing a burgundy-colored sweater. Then she saw a kid, a girl about her own age, who had blond hair pulled back into . . . a side ponytail!

Karen's heart sank. It couldn't be! But there weren't a lot of girls who wore that hairstyle. In fact, the only ones she knew were the girls in the Clovers.

What's more, only one of the Clovers had that particular shade of ash-blond hair.

Sidling over to the sleeping lump that was Amy, Karen nudged her. "Hey, Amy. Wake up. I just saw something horrible outside."

Amy opened one eye and glared at Karen. "It's probably a porcupine. Or a skunk. Just be still, and it will go away."

"It's no skunk," Karen whispered. "It's worse than a skunk. It's Holly Hudnut!"

"No way," said Amy, as she rolled over and went back to sleep.

Sure of what she had seen, Karen resumed her spying on the camper. A few minutes later, the door opened and out came Holly and her best friend, Brenda Wallace.

"Look at that tent over there," Brenda could be heard saying. She seemed to be staring right at Karen.

"Yuck," said Holly. "It looks like a giant toadstool. I'm glad *we* don't have to sleep on the ground. Last year when we borrowed Uncle Jack's camper, we stayed at a place where they didn't even allow tents. It was really nice there, too. They had a heated swimming pool and a room with video games. They even had cable TV hookups."

La-dee-dah, thought Karen. Even though she wasn't all that crazy about staying in a tent herself, Holly's attitude made her see red.

Karen turned around and nudged Amy again. "Listen," she hissed. "I'm not kidding. Holly's outside. And Brenda Wallace is with her. I just saw them."

Groggily, Amy pulled herself up and peered out the open tent flap. "I don't see anyone."

"They must have gone back inside. They were there a second ago."

"Naw," said Amy soothingly. "You just

had a nightmare, that's all. Go back to sleep, and in the morning they'll be all gone."

. . .

When Karen woke up, the blue camper was still there, hogging the view of the lake. The Venetian blinds that covered the camper's windows were pulled down, and the door was closed.

Were Holly and Brenda really inside?

The memory of what she had seen and heard the night before still seemed vivid, but Karen couldn't be one hundred percent sure that she hadn't just been having a bad dream. She'd just to have to wait and see.

The floor of the tent was covered with a tangle of sleeping bags, backpacks, discarded clothes from yesterday, and miscellaneous junk. The sun must have been up for a few hours, because the tent had absorbed so much heat that it felt like a greenhouse. Quickly, Karen pulled on her warm-up pants and a T-shirt, grabbed her toothbrush, and headed outside.

Mr. Danner had started the stove, and Jan was already busy putting together their breakfast. She had found some powdered eggs, powdered milk, and flour in Amy's supplies. Amy was helping her mix the pancake batter.

"Beth and Sara found a blueberry patch and went to pick some berries so I can add them to the pancake mix," Jan explained to Karen.

When Karen returned from brushing her teeth, the twins were back. Sara held a small plastic container with a couple of handfuls of wrinkly-looking berries in the bottom. "I guess they're kind of dried out," she apologized.

Jan took one of the berries and bit into it. "They sure are."

Beth held out her plastic bucket proudly. "It wasn't a total waste, though. Look what I got."

Jan peered inside. A large brown toad regarded her with bug-eyed curiosity. "Yech! I hope you didn't pick berries after you touched that. It's disgusting."

"It is not," Beth contradicted her. "You just don't appreciate nature. This is one great toad! Besides," she added with a giggle, "I had to bring it back to show you, because it reminded me of someone. Guess who?"

"The frog prince," suggested Karen. "Maybe if you kiss it, it will turn into a handsome rock star."

Sara frowned. It wasn't a good idea to suggest things like that to Beth. She could never pass up a dare. "Don't kiss it, Beth. Please," she begged.

"You guys are sick," Beth shot back. She picked up the toad and cradled it gently in her cupped hands. "Actually, I was thinking that it looked a little like Holly Hudnut."

Amy studied the toad. Holly was pretty, there was no getting around that. But come to think of it, there was something toadlike about the smirking expression she always wore. "You know, you're right!" Amy exclaimed.

Karen glanced nervously in the direction of the camper. Now was the time to warn the others of what she had seen.

But Amy beat her to it. "You'll never guess what Karen dreamed in the middle of the night," she said. "She had this idea that Holly and Brenda were in that camper over there."

Everybody laughed.

Okay, thought Karen. If that's the way

you want to be, wait and see for your-selves.

She shrugged her shoulders and went over to help Jan, who was having a tough time cooking pancakes over their little camp stove. She couldn't seem to get the flame hot enough, so by the time the insides of the pancakes were cooked, the outsides were hard and a little charred-looking. Fortu-nately, Mr. Danner's food stash included a bottle of pancake syrup, and once that was slathered over the pancakes, they didn't taste too bad.

Amy examined the gigantic bottle of syrup. Then she stole a glance at her fa-ther to check his reaction. "I can't wait to hear what Mom says when I tell her about all this junk food we're eating."

The other Stars kept their eyes on their plates. Amy was starting in on her father awfully early. At last, Jan decide to play peacemaker. "Maple syrup may be sweet," she put in, "but it isn't exactly junk food. It's natural. The Indians ate it all the time. They even put it in stews and stuff."

She was about to go on, when she heard an all-too-familiar voice behind her.

"Yuck!" it squealed. "Can you believe it? What are *they* doing here?"

"This is gross!" chimed in a chorus of supporting voices. "Outrageous! Weird!"

Jan and Amy turned and found themselves face-to-face with the Clovers.

"Uh-oh," said Jan.

Karen's heart sank. "I knew it wasn't a nightmare!" she said out loud, then clapped her hand over her mouth. This was even worse than she'd thought last night. *All* the Clovers were here. Not just Holly and Brenda, but Mary Rose Gallagher, Roxanne Sachs, and Sue Pinson, too.

Holly was the first to recover from the surprise.

"Oooh, aren't they disgusting," she said, turning up her button nose at the contents of the Stars' plates. "Looks like lard cakes." It was hard to tell whether she was referring to the breakfast or to the Stars themselves.

"I agree," said Brenda. "It's really *raucous.*"

"Raucous" was the Clovers' new favorite word. Mr. Gill, the chorus teacher at school, was always accusing the kids of raucous behavior when they made too much noise. The Clovers had taken up the word and used it to mean "gross" or "tacky" or "disgusting," or whatever they felt it should mean at the moment.

Jan didn't miss a beat. She turned to Beth and said casually, "You'd better check on that toad. I think it may have turned into its look-alike." Beth started giggling, and Holly waited patiently for her to stop. She was like a teacher who insisted on having the total attention of the class before she spoke.

"What are you guys doing here?" she challenged them.

"We could ask you the same question," Amy pointed out.

Holly sniffed. "Don't be ridiculous. We always come to Lake Laverne. We've been planning this trip for weeks. You Stars are just copycats."

"We are not," protested Amy indignantly. "We didn't know anything about your trip, or we wouldn't have come. Besides," she added weakly, "it's a free country. We can camp anywhere we want."

Amy wanted to bite her tongue. She knew

she sounded defensive, and she hated herself for it. After all, the Stars had arrived first. How could they possibly have known that Holly and Brenda would end up camping right next to them?

Amy was trying to think of a good putdown, when her dad spoke up. "Aren't you going to introduce me to your friends?" he asked.

None too happily, Amy did.

Holly's smile was so fake it looked as if her face might crack down the middle. "Nice T-shirt, Mr. Danner," she said insincerely.

Amy felt mortified. Her dad was wearing a Mickey Mouse T-shirt, just like the one she had. Not that she cared what Holly Hudnut thought, but she wished her dad wasn't such an easy target for Holly's wisecracks.

Holly's eyes were busy, checking out the Stars' clothes and camping gear. She looked ready to deliver her opinions on what she saw, but she didn't get the chance. Mrs. Hudnut had emerged from the camper and was calling Holly to come help get breakfast ready.

Mr. Danner shrugged his shoulders and

grinned ruefully. "Why do I feel as if we've just had a visit from Princess Di and Fergie?"

Everyone laughed, including Amy.

Over at the Hudnuts' campsite, Holly and the other Clovers were helping Mrs. Hudnut set the picnic table with a blue-and-white-checked tablecloth, real china, and glassware. When the Hudnuts went camping, they went in style. A cart loaded with electrical appliances—a toaster oven, a juicer, and some things Amy didn't even recognize—was plugged into an outlet on the side of the camper.

Mr. Hudnut, meanwhile, was busy adjusting two big stereo speakers that were mounted on the camper's roof, front and back. When he got the adjustment the way he wanted it, he flipped a switch. Blasting from the speakers came the strains of one of those easy-listening radio stations, playing a medley of oldie-but-goldie rock tunes, arranged for lots of violins.

"They're not going to get away with blasting that Muzak at us all day," Mr. Danner announced. "I'm going to go ask them to turn it down."

"Daddy, no!" said Amy automatically. All

she needed was for her dad to get into a fight with Holly's dad.

"Of course I'm going to," Mr. Danner said. "We don't have to put up with that."

He strode over to the blue camper. At first, he and Mr. Hudnut seemed to be arguing, but soon Mrs. Hudnut came out of the camper carrying a fresh pot of coffee. She poured a mugful for Mr. Danner, and soon the three adults were seated at the picnic table, having a friendly discussion.

Amy couldn't decide whether that was a good sign or not. She just wished she could keep her dad and the Clovers in two separate compartments of her life. Having them come together made her uncomfortable.

"Don't worry," Beth said, reading Amy's mind. "We won't let the Clovers ruin our good time. We'll just ignore them. Right?"

"That's right. And anyway, it's a beautiful day," Sara added, trying to look on the bright side. "I bet it's going to be eighty degrees by noon. We can go down to the lake and swim." She pointed toward the small sand beach, just visible through the pine trees. "Look, there's a couple of families down there already. It'll be great."

They all dug into their packs until they

found their swimsuits, then they marched off to the women's dressing room, to take their morning showers and change for the beach.

The dressing room was strange. There was a row of individual cubicles for changing clothes, but the showers were in a big area separated only by plastic curtains. Karen noticed a small spider on her side of the plastic curtain that separated her shower from Amy's. She kept her eye on it as she lathered up, hoping it wouldn't run down to the floor and crawl over her bare toes.

"Talk about rotten luck," Sara said, raising her voice so she could be heard from the shower at the far end. "Who would have thought the Clovers would show up at this very campground?"

"I guess it isn't such a big coincidence," Jan yelled back. "Lake Laverne is a pretty popular spot. And this is one of the most popular campgrounds on the lake. In the summer, you couldn't get a campsite like ours without reserving way in advance."

"I still think it's unfair!" Amy complained. This weekend was turning out to be just as much of a disaster as she'd feared.

Jan was washing her hair and had managed to get shampoo in her eyes. "Ouch, that stings!" she yelped. She jumped out of the shower area and started feeling around blindly on the bench where she had left her towel. "Hey, guys, come on," she pleaded. "Where'd you put my stuff?"

"We didn't do anything—" Sara began.

"Yikes!" Amy interrupted her. She had stepped out of the shower and was surveying the row of dressing stalls. "Everything's gone! Someone stole our things! What are we going to do?"

From outside they heard Holly's high-pitched giggle. Soon it was joined by Brenda's unmistakable braying laugh. Then Mary Rose, Roxanne, and Sue joined in the chorus.

"Wait till I get my hands on those guys!" Beth exploded. She was ready to charge out after them, but Sara pulled her back. "You can't go out like that!"

None of them could. That was the problem.

"Maybe we should just wait until somebody else comes in," Jan suggested. "Then we can ask her to bring us a robe or something."

They waited five minutes or so, but no one showed up.

"I've had it," Beth said finally. "I'm not going to waste my day hiding in here. There's got to be something I can put on."

Everyone looked around the big dressing room, but it was completely bare. Then Beth had a brainstorm. She pointed to the paper-towel dispenser on the wall.

While Sara turned the handle, Beth started wrapping the unrolling paper toweling around herself. "See," she said hopefully. "It's like a sari. As long as I keep my arms at my sides to hold it up, I'll be okay."

She peered around the entrance to the dressing room and spotted their clothes in a big pile by a picnic table just a few yards away. "Here goes," she said, making a dash for it.

The Clovers were still waiting outside. As Beth streaked past them, they whistled and screeched. "Beth's bare na-ked!" shouted Mary Rose, loud enough to alert the entire campground.

"I see Frisco, I see France," chanted Holly. "Beth's not wearing underpants!"

Of course, Beth wasn't exactly naked, but people stared just the same. A family of campers who happened to be using the water fountain outside the changing rooms grinned and pointed as Beth scuttled to the picnic table, grabbed an armful of bathing suits and towels, and hightailed it back inside, taking quick, choppy steps in an effort to hold up her paper sari as she ran.

"You were great!" said Jan, as Beth passed out the suits to the other girls. "I never would have had the nerve."

Beth was as red as a beet, but she felt triumphant at the same time. "Did you see the look on the faces of those people at the water fountain?" she laughed.

· · ·

Back at the campsite, Beth dug out her personal tape player, her headset, and the tapes she'd brought with her. She and Sara made their own cassettes from borrowed records and the radio, so they had quite a collection.

Beth picked out a King Zero tape and slid it into the player, then carefully pushed the Play button. The machine was new and more complicated than the Walkman she'd passed on to her brother Jeffrey. For one thing, it could record as well as play. So far, she'd managed to erase two tapes by accidentally pushing the Record button while she was carrying the tape player in her back pocket.

While the others were getting their stuff together to take down to the beach, she sat down under a tree and pretended to listen to the music. But she was really thinking about a way to get even with Holly.

A few minutes later, Mr. and Mrs. Hudnut came out of the camper and headed off in the direction of the campground office. Beth couldn't help noticing that they had left the door open. Wide open. The Clovers were nowhere in sight, either. It was just too tempting.

"Hey, look!" she whispered, when Amy came out of the tent with her stuff. "Want to sneak inside the Hudnuts' camper? Maybe we can short-sheet the Clovers' beds. That would get even with them."

"Are you crazy? What if the Hudnuts come back?"

"So what?" Beth shrugged. "The door is open, right? We'll just say we were looking for Holly."

Something told Amy it wouldn't be that easy. But she, too, didn't want the Clovers to get away with the stunt they had pulled. There had to be a payback. "Okay," she said. "Let's go."

Inside, the camper looked like the house of the Seven Dwarfs. The furniture was all just a little bit smaller than normal, and it was covered with flowered chintz cushions that matched the curtains. On top of one of the suitcases was a big pile of stuffed animals. Someone—Holly, they imagined—must have brought her entire collection along.

The camper's walls were hung with souvenir plaques, some with pictures of scenery and others with cute sayings on them, like GENIUS ON BOARD and I ♥ CAMPING and I BRAKE FOR WHALES.

Beth made a quick inspection of the place. "There's a little room above the driver's seat," she said. "That must be where Holly's folks sleep. But what about everyone else?"

"I think I know," Amy said. She climbed up a ladder that was resting against some cabinets and pulled on one of the knobs. The door slid down, opening into a bed, all made up with sheets, a pillow, and a plaid blanket.

"That's neat," exclaimed Beth. "It's just

like an upper berth on a train. You know, like you see in old movies." While she talked, Beth was hard at work short-sheeting the beds.

"Are you sure we should do this?" Amy asked nervously. "Aren't we trespassing or something?"

Beth rolled her eyes. "It's just a joke. And if you're so worried about getting caught, then you'd better give me a hand. It'll go faster that way."

They were working on the fifth bed, when they heard voices outside. "Good grief!" whispered Beth. "It sounds like Holly and Brenda! We'd better hide!"

Hurriedly, she finished the last bed and dived under the table in the breakfast nook, where she was hidden from view by the pine benches.

Amy felt paralyzed. Hiding seemed dumb. What if Holly found them there? How would they ever explain why they were crouched under the table? On the other hand, she couldn't think of a plausible explanation for why she and Beth had pulled down all the beds. At the last minute, she ducked under the table too.

Squeezed in next to Beth, Amy had a view

of Holly's and Brenda's legs as they paced around the trailer, looking for something. "Oh, here they are!" Holly squealed. "Brucie Bear was wearing my sunglasses!"

Beth realized that Brucie must be one of Holly's stuffed animals. She snorted and clapped her hand over her mouth.

Fortunately, Holly and Brenda didn't notice the noise.

"Look at this!" Holly was saying. "The beds aren't closed up. I told Mary Rose to do it. She's such a slob sometimes."

"You said it," Brenda agreed. "She can be a real pig."

Holly laughed. "At least she doesn't have a tacky suitcase. Did you see Roxanne's? I mean, really. It looks like an old gym bag!"

"Right," said Brenda. "And did you see Sue's pajamas last night? They were so babyish!"

"Yeah. Flannel p.j.'s with little yellow chicks on them. Ugh!"

At last Holly and Brenda got tired of cutting up the other Clovers and headed back for the beach.

As soon as they were gone, Amy and Beth scrambled out from under the table. "Can you believe that!" said Amy. "I wonder what the other girls would say if they knew what Holly and Brenda really think about them?"

"That would be ver-r-ry interesting," said Beth mysteriously. "Maybe someday we'll get to find out."

Amy was puzzled, but this was no time to ask Beth for an explanation. Glancing out the camper door, she could see Mrs. Hudnut a few dozen yards down the trail, getting a drink at the water fountain. "Let's get out of here while the getting's good," she said, half pushing Beth toward the door.

◀ 4 ▶

Can You Canoe?

By the time the Stars got down to the lake, the Clovers had staked out the best spot on the handkerchief-size beach. Holly was playing Whitney Houston tapes at top volume on a big boom box. Brenda had brought her camera and was hopping around pretending that she was a professional photographer, snapping pictures of the other Clovers as they modeled their bathing suits.

Beth was all for kicking sand on their blanket, but the other girls wouldn't let her.

"That's kid stuff," said Jan. "Let's just ignore them." She plunked the Stars' blanket down at the opposite end of the beach.

But ignoring the Clovers was not easy. Soon Holly's voice could be heard loud and clear. "Do you know how the Stars got their name?"

Brenda responded with her little whinnying laugh. "Sure. It's because they have pointed heads."

"Here's another one," Holly went on. "What has five trillion freckles and a combined IQ of ten?"

Brenda and Roxanne Sachs answered in unison: "The Greenfields!"

"You said it." Mary Rose laughed. "The Gruesome Twosome!"

"That's it," Beth muttered. "I don't have to take that." She watched as Brenda aimed her camera at Roxanne, who struck a pose with one hand on her thrust-out hip.

"Roxanne Sex!" Beth boomed out. "They call her that because she thinks she's so sexy, but she's not."

Sara groaned. Everyone knew that Roxanne hated her nickname. She was pretty tough, too. Even the boys in class usually didn't call her that to her face.

Sure enough, Roxanne was striding across to their blanket, kicking up a ton of sand with each step she took. "Who said that?" she demanded.

Beth was on her feet in a flash. "I did. Want to make something of it?"

"I sure do!"

Beth didn't really want to fight. But she wasn't about to be the first to back down. The two girls stood face-to-face—or rather they would have been face-to-face, except that the top of Beth's head barely came to Roxanne's chin.

Fortunately, at that moment Mr. Danner showed up and interrupted the argument. "Ladies, please!" he said, smiling as though the confrontation were a big joke. "This round is over. Retire to your corners until the bell rings for round two."

Roxanne made a face at the dumb joke. But when Mr. Danner stared back at her, she muttered, "Okay, right," and headed for the Clovers' blanket.

"Since you kids obviously don't get along," Mr. Danner said, "why hang around here? Look, I have an idea. We can rent canoes. It's not far from here. We can walk there and get a couple of them. Just because your buddies over there aren't interested in anything but sitting around showing off for each other, that doesn't mean you have to do the same. Right?"

"Right," agreed Jan. "I vote to get out of here."

"Me too," seconded Amy. Even if it was her dad's idea, she was all in favor of putting some distance between herself and the Clovers.

The others nodded in agreement.

• • •

Ten minutes later, they were standing on the dock of the White Birch campground, choosing up canoes.

"Do any of you girls know anything about canoeing?" the lifeguard in charge of rentals asked.

Jan nodded. "I won a badge at camp last summer."

"I know about canoeing too," Amy put in. "I went to wilderness survival camp in Canada. We did whitewater and everything."

The lifeguard looked impressed. With her crazy jewelry and far-out hairstyle, Amy didn't look like the outdoors type. Even now, with her bathing suit, she was wearing earrings she had made from a set of jacks and a denim shirt decorated with rhinestones from a necklace she had bought at a garage sale.

Actually, Amy *wasn't* the outdoors type, but her mother was. Mrs. Danner happened to have a thing about girls being self-reliant, and after the divorce, she had insisted on sending Amy away to a camp that offered a "survival experience" in the Canadian woods.

Amy had hated the place at first. It was bad enough that her dad had moved out. She felt that on top of everything, her mother was punishing her by sending her away.

Almost against her will, she had ended up enjoying the summer. A lot of the kids at camp had parents who were divorced, and Amy had made quite a few friends. She had come home knowing a lot about canoeing and even more about acting confident, even though inside she sometimes felt just as lonely and confused as she had right after her parents split up. In just two months, she had grown up a lot.

The trouble was, her dad didn't seem to notice the change. Whenever they got together, he wanted to kid around the way they used to, when she was just a little kid.

While the lifeguard was handing out life vests and assigning places in the two canoes they had chosen, Mr. Danner was selecting a kayak-shaped rubber boat for himself. Amy went over to him and said in a low voice, "Look, Dad. It's okay. You don't have to come out with us. We're not babies, you know."

"I know that," said Mr. Danner. He looked hurt. "I just thought I'd have a little fun too. Of course, if you don't want me around . . ."

Jan and the twins were already loaded into the first canoe, ready to shove off. Amy didn't know what to do. Her dad was wearing a pair of big blue swim goggles he had rented. He said they were to protect his contact lenses. Between the goggles and his swimming trunks, with their blinding floral-print pattern, he looked ridiculous, Amy thought—sort of like Charlie Tuna goes Hawaiian.

"Forget it," she said, defeated. She strapped on her life vest, then went over and got into the second canoe.

Mr. Danner, meanwhile, was having quite

a struggle getting himself launched in the little kayak. He was a big man, with muscular arms, and as he lowered himself from the dock into the lightweight rubber boat, it lurched dangerously.

Karen laughed. "You remind me of Popeye in that tiny boat."

"Right," he said. "Like in the song." And he sang out, very quickly:

"I'm Popeye the sailor man, *toot toot,*
I'm Popeye the sailor *man* . . .
I love to go swimmin'
With bow-legged women—"

"*Dad*-dy!" Amy said, mortified.

Mr. Danner saw the embarrassment on his daughter's face and looked contrite. "Don't worry, kitten," he reassured her. "I'll be on my good behavior from now on. No more foolishness."

"Fat chance," Amy muttered under her breath.

There was something about boats that always brought out her dad's urge to clown around. Normally, she would have laughed at that song, but not in front of the other girls. The trouble was, they were all laughing as if it was a big joke.

Jan and the twins were the first to glide away from the dock, powered by the smooth, even strokes of Jan's paddle.

Back on the pier, Karen was studying the best way to get into the canoe she was to share with Amy. For a minute or two, Mr. Danner's joking around had almost made her forget that she was nervous about actually going out on that huge lake in this small, unstable-looking fiberglass canoe. Now she had no choice but to leave the security of dry land. Very cautiously, she sat down on the edge of the dock and planted both feet in the middle of the canoe.

"Good grief," said Amy. "Just get in. You act as if you were never in a boat before." She was so preoccupied, worrying about what the others thought of her father, that she had no patience for Karen's problems.

"I never *was* in a boat before," Karen said.

Amy could hardly believe it. "It's perfectly safe. I mean, you do know how to swim, don't you?"

Karen nodded uncertainly. She had passed her beginner's test in a class at the Y. But that was in the Y swimming pool. "I never swam in water like this before," she said, peering over the side of the canoe. "It's all . . . dark."

"Don't worry," Amy reassured her. "You swim the same way in a lake as you do in a pool. Besides, you're wearing a life vest. You couldn't sink even if you wanted to."

Logically, Karen knew all that. But her queasy stomach didn't seem to be getting the message. Holding her breath, she pushed herself off the dock and plopped onto the front seat of the canoe, which rocked sickeningly in reaction to her sudden movement. Then, while Amy paddled, she sat stiffly in the bow, clutching the seat for dear life.

In the other canoe, Beth had taken over the second paddle. Together, she and Jan were moving smartly along, while Sara rode in the center, pretending she was Tiffany Vandermere on her way to meet Sean and his band of reformed pirates, who had dedicated themselves to rescuing travelers in distress. In no time at all, the canoe had rounded the little spit of land that marked the boundary of the White Birch campground, and Jan and the twins were headed back toward their own dock.

Struggling to keep up, Amy started yelling at Karen. "Don't just sit there! Don't let them beat us!"

Karen didn't want to be a party pooper. Obediently, she picked up her paddle and took a few timid strokes. She must not have been doing it right, though, because instead of moving the canoe forward, her paddling seemed to pull it to one side.

Amy started to giggle in spite of herself. "Forget it," she told Karen. "You're hopeless."

With a few powerful strokes, Amy drew closer to the other canoe and yelled a challenge: "Race you to the dock!"

Jan and Beth paddled harder, but their canoe was slightly bigger and heavier, and soon Amy was just a few feet behind them. As they neared the campground dock, Amy gave a few extra-hard pulls.

Jan, who was circling around, preparing to approach sideways, suddenly realized that Amy was going to touch the dock first. Abruptly, she gave a hard pull on her paddle too.

Now the two canoes were on a collision course. As they skimmed closer to each other, Amy shouted to Karen, "Okay, I need your help now. Backpaddle on your right."

Karen had no idea what Amy wanted her to do. Transfixed by the sight of the other canoe, which was headed straight for them, she plunged her paddle into the water and flailed away. The effect was the opposite of what Amy wanted. Instead of moving out of the way of the oncoming canoe, they were headed directly for it.

As the two canoes came together, Karen reached out instinctively to stop them from butting into each other. Unfortunately, she was so scared that she grabbed the side of the other canoe a lot harder than she intended, tilting it sideways.

"Hey!" gasped Sara as the cold lake water poured in on her. "No fair!" Playfully, she reached out and gave Amy and Karen's canoe an answering shove.

Suddenly, Karen realized that she had accidentally started something she wasn't prepared to finish. In a panic, she stood up and started climbing toward the back of the canoe. It was completely irrational, but somehow she felt she'd be safer sitting back there with Amy.

Instead, her sudden move was the last straw. The canoe rolled under her, like a whale going down for a dive, and the next thing Karen knew, she and Amy were being dumped into the lake.

Beth had been wanting to swim all day, even if it was late in the season. Seeing Karen and Amy go in the water, she stood up, yelled "A-ban-don ship!" and jumped in after them. Sara and Jan gave up bailing and looked at each other. "Why not?" said Jan with a shrug.

"Let's go on the count of three," said Sara. "One, two, thu-reee!"

They both hit the water at the same instant. "Whew!" gulped Jan. "It's cold!"

"You said it!" Sara agreed. "It's not too bad, though. Once the first shock wears off."

Except for Karen, everyone was happy to get wet. Jan retrieved the paddles and dumped them into her half-submerged canoe. The other girls were chasing one another around the overturned hulk of Amy and Karen's canoe, laughing and shrieking.

Mr. Danner, farther out on the lake, saw the commotion and came charging to the rescue in his ridiculous rubber boat. "I'm coming, girls," he shouted.

At almost the same moment, Karen made a humiliating discovery. She was bobbing around in her life vest, waiting to be rescued, when suddenly her feet touched something hard. It was the bottom of the lake!

"I guess this water isn't as deep as I thought," she yelled, standing upright in the chest-deep water.

Beth dog-paddled to her side. "I wish you could have seen yourself climbing into the back seat," she said.

Karen laughed. Her fears had been pretty silly.

Behind them, from the direction of the beach, Brenda Wallace's whinny informed them that the entire scene had been witnessed by the Clovers. In fact, not just the Clovers. The manager of the campground and Mr. Hudnut had come running down to the dock too.

Once he saw that the girls were in no danger, Mr. Hudnut took a small camera out of his pocket and started snapping pictures madly. "Why doesn't your crowd ever do stuff like this?" he said to Holly, who had joined him on the dock. "All you ever do is sit around thinking up things you want to buy."

Eventually, with Mr. Danner's help, the

Stars managed to get the canoes out of the water and safely tied to the campground dock, where they could remain until it was time to return them. The Clovers, meanwhile, had gone back to their blanket where they sat giggling.

Deep down, Amy had to admit she'd enjoyed the canoe race and dunking. But having the Clovers for an audience made her self-conscious all over again. Then, as if being watched by Holly and the others wasn't enough, her dad did something so dumb she could hardly believe it. Still wearing his dumb goggles and holding the bright-yellow paddle in one hand, he rested his free arm on Amy's shoulder and struck a pose. "How about taking our picture, Howie?" he said to Mr. Hudnut.

That was too much. Not only did her dad look silly in his flowered swim trunks, but Amy was soaking wet and still wearing her ugly orange life vest. All she needed was for the Clovers to get their hands on a snapshot of her and her dad looking like a pair of nerds.

"No way!" she said, slipping out of his grasp.

Mr. Hudnut had already focused his

camera and was aiming it in their direction.

"Come on Amy, be a sport!" said Mr. Danner.

"Forget it! Just leave me alone, all of you!" All she knew was that if her dad was going to make a fool of himself, she didn't want any part of it. Tears of embarrassment welling up in her eyes, she strode off toward the campsite.

Mr. Danner shrugged his shoulders and looked puzzled. "What did I do?"

The other girls just stared at each other. Even if they had wanted to explain, they couldn't exactly do it with Mr. Hudnut around.

Finally, Beth spoke up. "Don't get upset, Mr. Danner. It's no big deal. I guess Amy's just camera shy."

◀ 5 ▶
The Big Rock Candy Mountain

"I think Amy kind of overreacted," Sara said later as she and the other girls changed into their clothes in the dressing room. "I mean, there was no reason to get all upset."

"She'll be okay," said Jan. "I tried to talk to her while you guys were in the tent getting your stuff. She just wants to be by herself for a while."

"I guess it's all my fault," volunteered Karen. "If it weren't for me, we wouldn't have ended up capsizing the canoes right in front of Holly and the other Clovers."

"I don't think that's Amy's problem," said Beth. "Anyway, it wasn't all your fault that we ended up in the water. I went in on purpose."

"So did I," said Jan and Sara in unison.

This time, the girls were taking no chances on being victims of another raid by the Clovers. Beth was perched on the top of a row of lockers, where she had a good view out of the bank of windows that ran along the top of the dressing room. From her high seat she peered down at Karen. "It is hard, though, to see how anyone could get seasick in a canoe. I never heard of that before."

"I couldn't *help* it," Karen protested. "I warned you guys I wasn't good at this outdoor stuff. Then when Amy kept yelling at me to back-pedal, I panicked. How can you back-pedal in a boat, for goodness' sake?"

"Back*paddle,*" explained Sara. "Not pedal."

"Oh," said Karen vaguely.

Beth pulled an imaginary chain, as if turning on a light bulb above Karen's head. "I thought you were supposed to be the brain of this group," she said, chuckling.

Karen looked almost pleased with herself. Being ditsy was one thing she didn't mind being accused of once in a while. Sometimes she got tired of always being the smart one.

"I think Amy's real problem is that she's embarrassed about her dad," Jan put in. "At least we're her friends. But having the Clovers around is just too much. You can bet that when we get back to school they'll never stop teasing her. I mean, he did look kind of goofy out there."

"I think Mr. Danner is nice," said Sara.

"Me too," said Karen. She started combing the knots out of her silky blond hair. "But I know how I feel when my friends meet my parents. I always feel sort of embarrassed, even though I *know* there's no reason to be."

"Still," said Sara, "I'd rather have Mr. Danner for a father than Mr. Hudnut. All *he* does is complain that Holly doesn't appreciate all the stuff she's got. It isn't worth having things if you have to go around appreciating them all the time."

"Speaking of Holly's dad," Jan said, "we've absolutely got to think of some way to get back at Holly and her buddies for stealing our clothes."

"Oh, don't worry," Beth said a bit mysteriously. "They'll get theirs when the time is right."

Before the others could ask Beth what she meant, Amy came in, looking like her old self again. "I'm sorry I freaked out like that," she said. "Anyway, I thought that tomorrow we should go for a hike up Mount Jasper. My dad really wants to go, so I thought we could humor him. If you guys don't mind."

"Mind?" said Jan. "Of course not. I like hiking."

"Sounds good to me, too," said Karen. After all, hiking was just walking, right? It wouldn't be like canoeing, where they all knew what they were doing except her.

That evening, Mr. Danner announced that he thought they'd had enough of survival food, so he drove them to the nearest grocery store to stock up on hot dogs, hamburger meat, coleslaw, and potato salad. Back in camp, he started a charcoal fire in the barbecue pit and they had a cookout.

After dinner, he suggested that they all get to sleep early. "That way we can get off to an early start in the morning," he said.

"I picked up some sandwich fixings and trail mix at the store. We'll pack a picnic lunch and make a day of it."

"At least we'll be away from the Clovers for a while," said Jan.

Mr. Danner made a face. "I'm afraid not. I was talking to the Hudnuts while you girls were in the shower room. I don't think Mrs. H. is exactly the outdoors type. She has some report for the Preservation Society that she's writing this weekend, so Mr. H. was looking for a way to keep the girls out of her hair. He wanted to know what there is to do around here, and I'm afraid I mentioned the trail up the mountain."

Everyone groaned.

"Are you serious?" Amy said. "If they go, I don't want to."

Mr. Danner gave her a sharp look. He seemed ready to tell her off, then he changed his mind. "I guess I goofed," he said with a shrug. "But Howie Hudnut probably would have gotten the same idea from the campground manager if he didn't hear it from me."

Amy looked around, hoping for support. No one else seemed ready to cancel the hike, though. "Okay," she said, "let's go anyway.

Maybe if we're lucky we won't even run into them."

• • •

That night, the girls sat in their tent, with the flap closed to keep out the chilly night air. Jan was trying to teach the others to play hearts. But between the bad lighting and Sara and Beth's fidgeting, they soon gave up the game.

They all looked over at the Hudnuts' camper. Two spotlights attached to the outside lit up the entire campsite. Through the window, they could see a portable color TV. No doubt all the Clovers were gathered around it.

"Imagine coming camping and not even missing your regular TV shows," Sara said scornfully.

"It's dumb," agreed Amy. "They might as well have stayed at home." But she couldn't help adding, "I wonder what station they're watching now?" Of all the Stars, she was the only confirmed couch potato.

"The Clovers make me so mad," said Jan. "We've got to think of some way to get back at them for stealing our clothes. We can't let them get away with it."

"Maybe we could move the trail markers," Karen suggested.

"Right." Sara giggled. "We could change them so that they point off the edge of a cliff. Like Wile E. Coyote does to the Road Runner."

"What about putting something slimy in their beds?" suggested Karen. "Like a snake."

"Or putting cayenne pepper in their trail mix?" suggested Jan. Then she frowned. "I'm not sure I have any with me. And besides, there's no way of getting near their food. I don't think Mrs. Hudnut has left the campsite once since she got here."

Amy and Beth shared knowing glances. "Oh, yes she has! She went away *once*," Beth said, grinning like the Cheshire cat. "Didn't she, Amy?"

"So?" Jan demanded. "Did you *do* anything?"

Amy couldn't stand the suspense of keeping their secret any longer. "We short-sheeted their beds," she blurted out.

"You didn't!" Sara, Karen, and Jan said in unison.

"We almost got caught, too," Amy added. "Holly and Brenda came in while we were still there. They would have seen us hiding if they hadn't been so busy cutting up their so-called friends."

"I wonder when they'll notice," said Jan, lifting the flap over the tent's mesh window and peering out at the Hudnuts' campsite.

As if on cue, there was a wave of outraged squeals from the blue camper. Then came voices raised in argument. It was hard to tell exactly what was being said, but it sounded as if they were accusing one another of being the culprit.

"That'll teach them!" Sara said triumphantly.

But Amy looked disappointed. "The trouble is, they don't know we did it. They think it was one of them."

The others groaned, all except Beth. "Don't worry," she assured them. "Holly and Brenda have another surprise coming. One even Amy doesn't know about."

"That's not fair!" Everyone was exclaiming. "Come on! Tell us!"

But Beth just burrowed down into her sleeping bag. "You'll know when the time comes," she said. "Trust me. In the meantime, you're keeping me awake. Mr. Danner is talking about waking us up at the crack of dawn, in case you forgot."

Beth was one of those people with the ability to fall asleep instantly. She was already dead to the world, clutching her pillow to her chest. One by one, the others dozed off too, until only Karen lay awake, listening to the low whooping sounds coming from the trees just behind their campsite. She knew by now that the sounds were made by an owl, but they still sounded eerie. It was impossible to imagine noises like that being made by the cute, wise-eyed owls you saw in children's books and cartoons.

When she finally fell asleep, she dreamed that the earth had been invaded by a race of feathered aliens who looked just like owls. And since the owl-people came out only at night, for a long time the earthlings never even suspected that civilization was being threatened. Only Karen knew the owls' true identity, and to keep her from warning the rest of the world, the aliens had kidnapped her and were holding her in one of their secret hiding places, high in a giant tree. While they debated what to do about her, a committee of owl-people was gathered around, watching her.

Frantically, Karen wondered how she'd ever be able to get away. "I've got to escape," she kept saying over and over in her dream. "But I don't know how to fly. I don't even know how to back-pedal."

Suddenly one of the owl-people reached down and pecked her on the shoulder.

"Karen! Wake up!"

She sat up with a start.

It was Jan. The gray light of dawn was filtering through the open tent flaps, and the other Stars were crawling around the tent, hunting for clean clothes and for the sneakers they had taken off in the dark the night before.

"I thought you were a bunch of aliens that looked like owls," Karen said sleepily.

"Well, we're not," said Jan. "Now come on and get dressed. Amy, Beth, and Sara are all in favor of this idea of getting an early start. So I guess you and I have to get up, whether we're ready to or not."

"That's okay," said Karen. "Being kidnapped by aliens was no fun." Sleepily, she groped through her pack until she found underwear and a T-shirt. Then she pulled on her jeans from yesterday and ran a brush through her hair.

The other Stars were already outside at the picnic table, eating Sugar Snax and milk. Karen filled a bowl and managed to swallow a few bites. In fifteen minutes, they were all ready to start up the trail.

By the time Karen's normal wake-up time arrived, they had been hiking for almost two hours and were high up on the mountain. At an overlook where they had a good view of the lake and the trail below them, they stopped to rest and drink from their canteens. Mr. Danner had brought a harmonica along, and he pulled it out and started playing softly.

The sun had come up behind the lake, and the trees were bathed in an orangey-pink glow. Mr. Danner pointed to their ultimate destination, another hilltop, connected to the one they were standing on by a nearly level, pine-covered ridge.

"It's beautiful up here," Karen said, taking a deep breath. "No wonder people love to climb mountains. It seems as if we're a hundred miles away from civilization."

"There used to be black bears up here," Mr. Danner said. "Of course, that was years ago. There are hardly any bears left in this part of the state."

"How about alien invaders from outer space?" Jan said, giggling. "Karen thought she saw some last night."

"I don't know about that," he said, laughing.

As if in answer to his statement, a high-pitched quavering sound cut through the silence.

"See," said Mr. Danner. "Here come the aliens now."

Sara looked down over the cliff to a section of trail they had covered near the beginning of the hike. "Those aren't aliens," she said. "It's worse than that. It's the Clovers."

"Good grief!" said Amy. "Are they following us, or what? I thought by starting so early we'd be hours ahead of them."

"Don't be paranoid," Mr. Danner said. "Anyway, they're still pretty far behind us. It's just that the sound of that squawk box they're carrying travels far out here in the woods. If we move right along, we can probably get there and have our picnic before they arrive."

"Then let's go," Amy urged.

• • •

They started across the ridge trail, moving at a brisk pace. Karen was feeling proud of herself. Maybe she couldn't paddle, but at least she could keep up with the others today.

Then, suddenly, the trail reached a spot where the woods ended abruptly, and she and the others found themselves standing on the edge of a chasm. About fifty feet below, a fast-running stream tumbled across some mean-looking rocks. Ahead, the path continued across a swinging footbridge.

Karen hadn't thought much about the bridge when Mr. Danner mentioned it on their first night at the campground. Even now, at first glance, it didn't look too bad. But when Amy stepped out onto the wooden walkway, the bridge sank under her weight and began to sway gently.

Karen felt her knees go weak. "You have got to be kidding!" she said. "I'm not going out on that!"

"It's perfectly safe," Mr. Danner insisted. "The trail club maintains it."

"Maybe, but I forgot to tell you something. I'm afraid of heights."

"Come *on,* Karen," Amy urged. "Just don't look down. Okay? Why make a big deal out of this? You've got to go across sooner or later."

"Oh, no I don't." Karen sat down on a rock. "I'll just stay here. This is a nice spot. I'll have my lunch here and wait for you until you come back."

Sara looked doubtful. "If Karen doesn't go across, I'm not sure I want to, either. It does look kind of scary."

"What's wrong with you guys!" Amy complained. "Only a wimp would be afraid of this bridge."

"Fine," said Karen. "If that's the way you want to be, then I'm a wimp."

"Okay, cool it," Mr. Danner ordered. "Amy, there's no reason to start name-calling just because some of your friends don't have as much experience with things like this as you do. Now, let's all take five, okay?"

He went over to Karen and sat down next to her. "You know, heights don't bother me. But I used to have this terrible phobia about elevators. Then the first job I got after college was on the twentieth floor of a sky-scraper. I almost didn't take it because I was scared to ride up in the elevator. But you know what worked for me? I would try

hard *not* to think of a white rhinoc-
eros. . . ."

Karen smiled weakly. "I've heard that
one. It's almost impossible *not* to think
about something once you're trying not to.
But I don't see how that's going to help me,"
she pointed out. "It just proves that I can't
not think about being scared of falling."

Mr. Danner scratched his head. "I guess
you're right." He reached into the pocket of
his shirt, pulled out his harmonica, and
played a few riffs. "Ever hear this one?" he
asked. "I used to sing it to Amy when she
was little.

" 'In the Big Rock Candy Mountain,
    you never change your socks,
Little streams of sody-pop come
    trickling down the rocks.
Oh, the shacks all have to tip their hats
    and railroad bulls are blind.
There's a lake of stew,
    and ginger ale too,
And you can paddle all around it
    in a big canoe
In the Big Rocky Candy Mountain.' "

Karen was listening to the words in spite
of herself. "I don't get it," she said. "What

are railroad bulls? And how can a shack tip his hat?"

"I think railroad bulls were the police who used to catch hoboes when they tried to hitch rides on freight trains," Mr. Danner explained. "But I'm not sure what shacks are. Anyway, there are more verses. My favorite one is the one that goes,

> " 'I'm bound to stay
> where they sleep all day,
> Where they hang the jerk
> who invented work . . .' "

"How does the rest of it go?" asked Karen when he stopped in midverse.

"Come on," said Mr. Danner. "We can learn the words as we cross the bridge."

"That's blackmail!" she protested.

Mr. Danner grinned sheepishly. "Well, sure. In a way."

"Okay," agreed Karen. "You win." No silly song was going to make her forget her fears, but Mr. Danner was trying so hard that she didn't want to let him down.

Mr. Danner went across the bridge first, booming out the lyrics of the song in his loud, deep voice.

Karen followed right behind him, trying

to concentrate on the song instead of on the way the bridge bounced and swayed under their feet with every step. At first, she kept her eyes riveted to the far end of the bridge. Then a bird flew underneath the bridge, and Karen instinctively looked down.

Her glance focused on the rushing stream at the bottom of the ravine, and her stomach did a flip-flop.

"Keep your eyes on the end of the bridge," Mr. Danner reminded her between verses.

By now all the other Stars were singing too, and Karen forced herself to join in. At least the song kept her friends from directing all their attention to her, waiting for her to freeze up.

After what seemed like an eternity, she realized that the bridge was sloping upward slightly. That meant she was more than halfway across. There was no point in going back now. And besides, she couldn't go back even if she wanted to—the other girls were right behind her.

While the others sang, Karen half closed her eyes and silently counted off ten more steps. Then, miraculously, her feet touched solid ground.

She was grateful that Mr. Danner didn't

make a big deal out of her accomplish-
ment. He just congratulated her with a
gentle pat on the shoulder, as if he'd known
all along she'd be able to get across.

◄ 6 ►
The Clovers Catch Up

Once they were across the swinging bridge, the rest of the hike was easy. The trail wound around the summit of Mount Jasper, through a forest of evergreens and thick, low berry bushes. The same stream that cut through the chasm crossed the path several times more, but it was much smaller now. At the last crossing, there wasn't even a log bridge. The water was so low that the Stars and Mr. Danner were able to make their way to the far bank by jumping from one boulder to another.

Just beyond, they found a picturesque mountain pond, complete with a beaver dam. Mr. Danner climbed around on the rocky hillside on the far side of the pond, and in a few minutes he had located the entrance to the Indian cave.

"This is really great," Sara enthused, when they all went inside to explore. "It's so big, you could almost live in here. Sean and Tiffany could hide out here too, to escape from her wicked uncle Morley, who's been trying to kidnap her for ransom."

"Forget Sean and Tiffany for a minute," snorted Beth. "That's a real beaver lodge in the middle of the pond. If we're lucky, we might see the beavers when they come out for a swim."

They all settled down near the mouth of the cave to eat their picnic lunches. After they finished, Mr. Danner took out his harmonica again. "I don't know any songs about beavers, so we'll have to make do with this one," and he started to sing an old Beatles song, "Rocky Raccoon."

An hour later, they still hadn't seen any beavers.

"You know who else hasn't shown up?" Jan pointed out. "The Clovers. I wonder what happened to them."

"Maybe they got lost," suggested Sara hopefully.

"I bet they were afraid to cross the swinging bridge," said Karen. Now that she had conquered her fear, she almost enjoyed the thought of Holly being too much of a chicken to get across.

Amy hadn't said much since the beginning of the hike. Even though her friends seemed to like her dad, she was still feeling uncomfortable about the way he was acting, playing runs on his harmonica and singing "Rocky Raccoon came into the ro-o-m" in his booming bass voice.

"I think I'll go back along the trail a little way and look for them," she said. She motioned to Beth. "Want to come?"

"Not me," sniffed Beth. "I don't care if they never show up."

The others seemed to agree, so Amy started down the path on her own. She was just as happy to be by herself.

Retracing her steps, Amy came to the spot where the stream cut across the trail for the last time. She didn't feel like jumping across the rocks again, so she sat down on the bank, resting her back against a big boulder as she tried to sort out her thoughts.

She had to admit that so far, everyone seemed to be having a good time but her.

After a while, she picked up some flat pebbles and started skimming them along the surface of a shallow pool formed where a tree had fallen in the path of the stream.

Plop, went one of the pebbles, making an especially satisfying sound as it hit the water.

Gr-onk, came a strange snuffling sort of noise from the other side of the big boulder.

Amy figured that Beth had changed her mind and was hiding behind the boulder, waiting to surprise her.

"You can't scare me," she called out.

The snuffling noise started up again.

"Beth? That is you, isn't it?"

Amy peered around the rock. A large black bear was standing on its hind feet on the opposite bank of the stream, not fifteen feet away from her.

In her wilderness survival camp, Amy had been told that bears don't have facial expressions, but she could have sworn that this one did. It looked surprised to see her. And a little confused, too. *What now?* it seemed to be thinking.

Amy knew exactly how the bear felt. She tried to remember what else she had been told about bears. Unfortunately, she couldn't remember any of the practical advice she'd been given. Should she try to climb a tree? Or would that just make the bear want to chase her? She thought she remembered one of the counselors at camp saying something about making noise, to warn the bear off. That didn't sound like such a good idea to her, though.

Finally, she decided to compromise. "Shoo, bear," she said, but in a voice that was practically a whisper.

The bear cocked its head to one side. It seemed interested. Or maybe it just couldn't remember the advice it had heard about what to do when meeting a person. Instead of going away, it dropped down on all fours and began nosing around the rocks, looking for something to eat.

Okay, Amy thought. That didn't work. So what next?

But before she could do anything, she heard loud crashing noises coming up the trail on the other side of the stream. Seconds later, the Clovers came into view. Holly was in the lead, followed by Brenda. And third in line was Mr. Hudnut, carrying several of the girls' day packs in addition to his own.

None of the Clovers seemed very happy.

"This isn't fair, Daddy. You didn't tell us the hike was going to be this long," Holly was whining. "There'd better be something to see up here."

There's going to be something to see, all right, Amy thought.

"Holly, look out," she called in a clear but calm voice. "There's a bear here."

The warning set off a buzz of conversation among the Clovers. Then Holly's voice rose above the others'. "It's just the Stars playing a trick on us. Don't fall for their tricks. Come *on*."

For once, the Clovers weren't so quick to follow Holly's orders. They hung back, caught up in argument over who was going to carry the lunch packs.

The bear twitched its ears at the sound of Holly's voice and stood up on its hind legs again to get a better view. The wind must have been blowing Amy's way, because she suddenly got a whiff of animal odor. Whew! The bear could have used a deodorant.

At that moment, things started happening very fast.

Holly saw the bear and let out a high-pitched sound—sort of an *eeek!* noise. Too scared to say anything else, she pointed in the bear's direction and jumped up and down, *eek*ing for all she was worth.

The bear curled its lip and snarled.

For the first time, Amy was really afraid. She remembered her counselor at camp saying that one thing you should never do is put a bear in a position where it feels trapped. But that was exactly what was happening. She was on one side of the stream crossing, and Holly was on the other. And Holly was so scared, dancing up and down and shrieking for all she was worth, that you could hardly blame the bear for thinking it was being attacked.

Amy's heart was pounding so hard that she was surprised the others couldn't hear it. Something else the counselor had told her flashed through her mind: "Remember, the bear is more scared of you than you are of it." I doubt that, Amy thought.

She was still trying to decide what to do, when a figure appeared on the trail just behind Holly. The newcomer was strolling along, singing happily, "Rocky Racco-o-o-on came into his ro-o-o-m . . ."

"Daddy!" Amy gasped in relief.

Hoping to catch up with Amy so that they could talk in private, Mr. Danner had taken a shortcut down a narrow trail that started behind the Indian cave and came along the opposite side of the stream. For most of the way, his path was hidden behind a high wall of rocks. He came out into the open quite suddenly, at Holly's rear.

He sized up the situation immediately, and in one smooth move, he scooped Holly up in his arms and set her down behind him. "Just stay calm, both of you," he told her and Amy, his voice at once strong and soothing. "Let's not give this old girl the idea that we're trying to corner her."

Amy felt herself relaxing a little. Now she knew everything was going to be all right. Even better, the bear seemed to think so too. After one more halfhearted snuffling noise, it dropped onto all fours and trotted off down the streambed, scrambling easily over the big rocks until it disappeared from sight.

Amy bounded across the stream to her dad's side, and he reached out with one arm and gave her a big hug. Holly was already hanging on to his other arm. "You saved me, Mr. Danner," she said a bit breathlessly. "It was just like a movie! You stood in front of me so that the bear would attack you first. . . . That was really a brave thing to do!"

"Let's not overdramatize," Mr. Danner said. "No doubt the bear would have left on its own once it had a good look at us."

• • •

When they all arrived at the pond where the other Stars were, everyone started talking at once. Amy thought she ought to be the one to tell the story to her friends. After all, she had seen the bear first, and it was her dad who'd come to help them.

But Holly kept interrupting. "Mr. Danner was the hero!" she gushed. "He saved me! He really did!"

Amy was relieved when Holly finally got tired of retelling the story and the Clovers settled down under a tree a few feet away to have their lunch.

Mr. Hudnut looked exhausted. "First you girls bickered all the way up here," he told the Clovers, "and now this! I've had it. Just don't dawdle over your picnic, okay? I want to start back soon." Shaking his head, he walked over to where Amy's dad was sitting and squatted down next to him.

"If you ask me"—Sara giggled—"that bear was right to be scared of Holly."

"Well, it makes me mad," muttered Amy. "Holly was the one who got the bear all excited in the first place. I tried to warn her, and she didn't pay any attention to me. Now she acts as if I wasn't even there. Just wait. By the time we get back to school, she'll have changed the story around so that she's the heroine."

"I know," sighed Jan. And she added, in a voice just loud enough for the Clovers to hear, "Those Clovers are so cranky, you'd think someone short-sheeted their beds last night."

Holly and the others looked over at the Stars suspiciously.

Beth grinned wickedly and, reaching into her day pack, pulled out her portable tape player. "I can do better than that," she said. "Remember how I had this with me when we sneaked into the camper?" she asked Amy. "Well, the Record button must have gotten pushed in when we were edged under the table. I lost part of King Zero, but what I recorded instead is pretty interesting."

She clicked on the recorder and turned the volume up. Holly's high, piping voice came out of the speaker, loud and clear. "... *I told Mary Rose to do it. She's such a slob sometimes.*"

"*You said it,*" Brenda's voice answered. "*She can be a real pig.*"

Over where the Clovers were sitting, there was consternation. "Hey!" Holly shouted. "Turn that thing off."

"That's right," seconded Brenda, "or I'll come over and make you turn it off!"

Brenda was halfway to her feet, when Mary Rose grabbed her arm and pulled her back down. "Not so fast," she said. "I think the rest of us want to hear this."

Beth ignored them and let the tape play on, all the way through Holly and Brenda's comments about Roxanne's tacky suitcase and Sue's pajamas. And more. By the time it finished, the Clovers were in an uproar.

"So you think I'm a pig?" Mary Rose challenged Brenda.

"I didn't mean it," Brenda pleaded. "It was just a joke. You know."

"It doesn't seem so funny to me," Roxanne put in.

Mr. Hudnut put aside his lunch and strode over. "That's it! I told you girls I couldn't stand to hear any more bickering. Let's get our things together and go. Right now!"

"But, Daddy," Holly protested. "It wasn't us. It was all their fault." She pointed in the direction of the Stars, who were hard at work packing their lunch things, their faces composed into masks of innocence.

"I don't care who started it," Mr. Hudnut said. "This is just the last straw. Let's get going."

The Stars watched in silence as the Clovers finished the last of their sandwiches and packed up. They were still arguing when they disappeared down the trail, heading back toward the campground, Mr. Hudnut following.

"You don't think that was too mean?" Sara said guiltily.

Jan shook her head. "I don't think so. Anyway, Holly and Brenda say things like that right to their friends' faces. I don't think the other Clovers were really that surprised."

"That's true," put in Karen. "They seem to enjoy fighting."

"The one thing that still bothers me," Beth said, "is that Holly got to see the bear and I didn't. She didn't even appreciate it."

Mr. Danner had rejoined the group in time to hear Beth's complaint. "There's nothing you can do about that," he said. "I don't think that bear will be coming back here today. But if you're quiet, you might still get a chance to see the beavers."

Beth, Sara, Jan, and Karen crept quietly through the grass to a good spot for watching the beaver dam. Amy stayed behind, sitting near her dad in the entrance to the Indian cave.

"I have a confession to make," she told him. "I was worried that my friends would think you were weird. But they don't. They really like you."

Her dad put his arm around her shoulders. "I was worried too," he said. "That's the only reason I hiked all the way back to the stream to find you. I was worried about you."

"You were?"

"Sure. Don't you think I could see you weren't having a good time on this trip? I keep wanting for us to have fun together, the way we used to. But I guess I didn't stop to think that maybe some of our old games would seem silly in front of your friends. Sometimes I forget that you're growing up. Besides, I know you're angry with me, and sometimes I just don't know what to do to make us friends again."

"Me? Angry?" But the truth of what her dad had said made the tears well up in Amy's eyes. "Of course I'm mad at you," she admitted. "You *divorced* us! You divorced me and Mom!"

He reached out and hugged her close. "I'm sorry, Amy. I really am. It's hard to explain, but sometimes there's just no other way. I didn't divorce you, though. You mustn't think that. I'm sorry we're living so far apart right now, but it just worked out that way. But I'll always love you just the same."

Amy wiped away a tear. "Me too, Dad." Then she had a thought that made her smile. "The funny thing is that when Holly decided you were her hero, that made me really jealous."

Mr. Danner ruffled Amy's flyaway hair.

"Don't worry about that," he promised. "If I'm going to be anyone's hero, it's yours. Is it a deal?"

"It's a deal."

• • •

A few minutes later, a fat, sleepy-looking beaver surfaced near its lodge and took a casual swim around the pond. Amy thought the sighting was pretty tame, compared to her run-in with the bear. But in some ways the beaver was more interesting to watch. It must have been used to seeing hikers, because after checking them out casually, it smacked its tail hard on the surface of the pond and dove, only to reappear a minute or so later in the company of two smaller beavers.

"Those must be its first-year kits," Beth said. She was so excited that she had to bite her tongue to keep from shouting for joy.

After about twenty minutes, the beaver disappeared into its lodge, and the Stars began their hike back to the campground. The trip down the hill went much more quickly than the hike up. Karen even crossed the swinging bridge without being more than just a little bit afraid.

When they reached the campsites, the big baby-blue camper was gone.

"I guess Mr. Hudnut had enough of a wilderness experience for one weekend," said Mr. Danner that evening as they sat around the campfire toasting marshmallows. "He and his wife must have decided to take the girls home early."

"I'm sure the Clovers didn't mind," Jan said. "They were upset that the campground didn't have cable TV."

"That's pretty silly of them," Karen said. "I can't imagine why the Clovers wouldn't like it here. I mean, they ought to learn to appreciate nature."

Everyone stared at her.

Karen felt herself blushing. "Okay, I admit I didn't always appreciate it either. But I learned, right? In two days, all the things I was scared of actually happened. And I survived! I even had a good time."

"I had a good time too," said Jan.

"Us too," said Sara and Beth together.

"Me too." Amy sighed. "But then, I should have known it all along. I mean, who wouldn't enjoy a camping trip with my dad and the greatest bunch of friends ever?"

Off in the distance, the owl started its evening song, but this time it seemed to be echoing Amy's words: *Who-o-o-o? Who-o-o-o? Who-o-o-o?*